STERLING CHILDREN'S BOOKS
New York

An Imprint of Sterling Publishing Co., Inc.
1166 Avenue of the Americas
New York, NY 10036

To Freya Elise, our newest star — L.H.
To BG, my ever-shining North Star — H.W.S.

Text © 2020 Leslie Helakoski
Illustrations © 2020 Heidi Woodward Sheffield

ISBN 978-1-4549-3013-6

Library of Congress Cataloging-in-Publication Data

Names: Helakoski, Leslie, author. | Sheffield, Heidi Woodward, illustrator.
Title: Are your stars like my stars? / by Leslie Helakoski ; illustrated by
   Heidi Woodward Sheffield.
Description: New York : Sterling Publishing Co., Inc., 2020. | Summary:
   "Helps children consider the colors of their everyday lives . . . and
   imagine how others around the world experience the very same things"--
   Provided by publisher.
Identifiers: LCCN 2019019073 | ISBN 9781454930136 (book / hc-plc with jacket
   picture book)
Subjects: | CYAC: Stories in rhyme. | Color--Fiction. | Perspective
   (Philosophy)--Fiction.
Classification: LCC PZ8.3.H4134473 Ar 2020 | DDC [E]--dc23_2019019073

Distributed in Canada by Sterling Publishing Co., Inc.
c/o Canadian Manda Group, 664 Annette Street
Toronto, Ontario M6S 2C8, Canada
Distributed in the United Kingdom by GMC Distribution Services
Castle Place, 166 High Street, Lewes, East Sussex BN7 1XU, England
Distributed in Australia by NewSouth Books
University of New South Wales, Sydney, NSW 2052, Australia

For information about custom editions, special sales, and premium and corporate purchases,
please contact Sterling Special Sales at 800-805-5489 or specialsales@sterlingpublishing.com.

Manufactured in China

Lot #:
2 4 6 8 10 9 7 5 3 1
10/19

sterlingpublishing.com

Design by Julie Robine

Lace patterns on pages 6, 7, 8,14,16, 29, 33 courtesy of the Lace Museum Detroit.
Images on page 7 from *361 Full-Color All Over Patterns* (978-0-486-40268-0)
and on page 21 from *Paisley Designs* (978-0-486-99882-4) courtesy of Dover Publications, Inc.

ARE YOUR STARS LIKE MY STARS?

by
Leslie Helakoski

Illustrated by
Heidi Woodward Sheffield

STERLING CHILDREN'S BOOKS
New York

We look at the world every day.
You and me.
Do we see the same things?
Do you see what I see?

When you squint at the sky,
do you see the same hue?
Deep, wide, and open.
Is your blue . . .

. . . like my blue?

When the sun gazes down,
shining yellow and bold.
Is it warm? Full of sparkle?
Is your gold . . .

. . . like my gold?

When you dig in the dirt,
planting seeds in the ground,
is it earthy and rich?
Is your brown . . .

. . . like my brown?

Do you splash in a puddle
when the world is washed clean?
Are the leaves fresh and bright?
Is your green . . .

. . . like my green?

When you stroll in an orchard,
do sweet smells fill your head?
Is the fruit bold and flashy?
Is your red . . .

. . . like my red?

Does your shadow grow long
as the sun starts to sink?
Are the clouds soft and rosy?
Is your pink . . .

. . . like my pink?

When your eyes are shut tight,
do you peek? Just a crack?
Is the night smooth and sleepy?
Is your black . . .

. . . like my black?

When you stare at the stars,
do you see the same light?
Does it glow in the darkness?
Is your white . . .

. . . like my white?

We look at each other every day.
You and me.

Do we see the same things?

Do I see what you see?